CARL'S MASQUERADE

Carl's Masquerade

ALEXANDRA DAY

FARRAR STRAUS GIROUX

New York

For Harold,
who loves costumes and lantern light,
and speaks Dog

———————————

Also by Alexandra Day

Carl Goes Shopping
Carl's Christmas
Carl's Afternoon in the Park

Thank you to my daughter Christina for cheerfully
modeling sundry creatures and lovely ladies,
and to Maureen and her mother

Library of Congress catalog card number: 92-8743
Published in Canada by HarperCollinsCanadaLtd
Color separations by Photolitho AG.
Printed and bound in the United States of America
by Berryville Graphics
First edition, 1992

The Carl character originally appeared in *Good Dog, Carl*
by Alexandra Day, published by Green Tiger Press

"We're going to a masquerade party, Carl. Take good care of the baby."

"Oh! They must be Beauty and
the Beast. Great costumes!
Go on in."

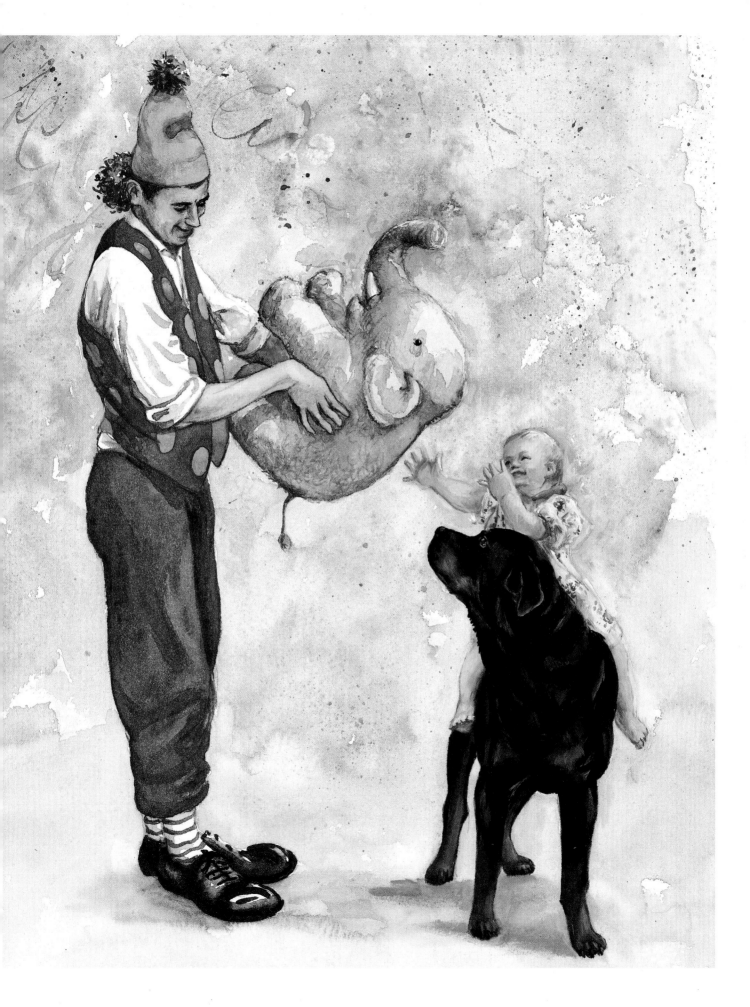

"I hope everything
went all right, Carl.
You're such a good dog."